WEAK AND WOUNDED

WEAK AND WOUNDED

Short Stories by

BRIAN JAMES FREEMAN

CEMETERY DANCE PUBLICATIONS

Baltimore

2019

For Norman Prentiss

With special thanks to Kathryn for helping me get through these once and for all; to Vicki Liebowitz for the care and feeding along the way; to Robert Brouhard, Serenity Richards, Brad Saenz, Rick Lederman, and Robert Mingee for the ground support; to Gail Cross, Robert Swartwood, and Tabitha Brouhard for the technical support; to Ron McLarty for the kind introduction; to Vincent Chong and Glenn Chadbourne for the remarkable artwork; and to Richard Chizmar, Julia and R.J. Sevin, Hans-Åke Lilja, and Mark Sieber for originally publishing several of these short stories in their earlier forms.

"Running Rain" originally appeared in Corpse Blossoms
edited by Julia Sevin and R.J. Sevin, published by Creeping
Hemlock Press, October 2005.

"Mama's Sleeping" is original to this collection.

"An Instant Eternity" originally appeared in Turn Down the
Lights edited by Richard Chizmar, published by Cemetery
Dance Publications, December 2013.

"Where Sunlight Sleeps" originally published
on the Horror Drive-In website edited by
Mark Sieber, April 2009.

"Marking the Passage of Time" originally appeared in
Shivers II edited by Richard Chizmar, published by
Cemetery Dance Publications, August 2003.

"Walking With the Ghosts of Pier 13" originally appeared in
Shivers edited by Richard Chizmar, published by Cemetery
Dance Publications, August 2002.

"A Mother's Love" originally appeared in Shining In the
Dark edited by Hans-Åke Lilja, published by Cemetery
Dance Publications, February 2018.

TABLE OF CONTENTS

INTRODUCTION

BY RON MCLARTY

THERE IS A GREAT TEMPTATION to discuss and describe each one of the astounding tales in Brian James Freeman's latest collection of short stories, but to do that would diminish the profound impact each one will have on readers who must discover the hope and the darkness themselves. What I can say is that each will leave you greatly moved and a bit disoriented, as a truth is uncovered, a hope is concealed, a terror is faced, a horror is revealed.

Everyone who aspires to art—to write, paint, compose—lives with both optimism and darkness. It seems to go with the territory especially if that territory encompasses serious fiction as Freeman's surely does. Nothing is easy. Things are never what they seem. For the writer, within a few pages into a story characters begin to assert themselves, and then as he finishes each session he wonders who is really writing this thing—him or the dude jogging in the rain.

But there is one thing you don't have to play over in your head and that is how great writing comes to be. It's one of the profound mysteries of art. It appears to move through some human beings like a soft breeze and arrive with a kind of perfection. Brian James Freeman is simply one of those human beings.

You will lose yourself in these pages.

RUNNING RAIN

THIS IS ONE OF THOSE perfect nights when he doesn't need the streetlights.

The world is bathed in the beautiful glow of the full moon, enough light to see for miles in every direction when he tops the hills.

The trees along the sidewalks sway in the winter wind and a dog howls somewhere in the distance, setting off the other dogs in the neighborhood like dominos toppling.

Tonight, he runs.

Running frees him from the pain of life, from the memories, from the nightmares.

Even with the bitter air nipping at his exposed skin, he runs.

He runs and he whispers the names: Benjamin, Amanda, Susan, Michael, Andy, Beth, Lauren, David.

He crosses back and forth from one side of the neighborhood to the other, and he doesn't stop when he reaches the place where the blacktop road ends and the woods begin.

He continues onto the dirt trail the kids keep clear every summer, the winding path along the river.

He runs and he memorizes the way the moonlight shimmers across the icy water.

The way the moonlight dances.

The first time he saw this river, he thought: Those waters are deeper and faster than they look.

That thought has troubled him ever since.

WHEN HE RETURNS HOME, HE is out of breath and his hands are shaking and his lungs are burning, but he's free.

He's been cleansed for another day.

He stands on the porch in the moonlight, bent over, his hands on his knees, and he gulps in the winter air.

He consumes the coldness, but a fire still rages inside of him.

×

"How was your run?" his wife asks from the kitchen as he locks the front door.

She's making hot chocolate. He can hear the water boiling on the stove.

This is their routine.

This is all they can talk about.

He stands in the living room, his heart still racing.

"Not bad. I took the path along the river," he says.

There's a sigh in the kitchen.

He knows what his wife is thinking, what she'll say, so why'd he tell her where he went? Why didn't he lie? Why can't he lie about this anymore?

He has deceived his wife before, but he can't stop himself from telling her this particular truth over and over again.

She may as well just say what she's going to say. Then they can get on with the fighting. It's the only time they talk to each other these days.

Each night they argue about him running near the river, but deep down, they're arguing about everything else.

Every secret. Every truth. Every lie. Every loss they share.

While he waits, he strips off his sweatshirt and unties his shoes.

Finally, with a trembling voice, his wife says: "Why don't you take a shower and have some hot chocolate?"

He doesn't respond.

Tonight, she's holding in the words she needs to release, but he can hear the tears well enough.

He stands in the shower, under the steady spray of water, and the pipes behind the walls whine like the pressure is so great they might burst.

The mirror fogs and the heat thaws his frozen flesh.

Goosebumps explode all over his body.

When the hot water hits his skin, he feels the night chill again.

It's deep inside of him; it's everywhere.

It's a coldness that will last for ages.

It's a coldness that devours him.

He imagines a block of ice inside his chest slowly melting, sending rivers of glacial water to the furthest reach of each of his limbs.

This thought reminds him of his father trying to explain to him the nature of a parent's love for their children.

He was merely a child then and his father had said: The waters of our heart are deeper and faster than they look.

His father was an educated man, but he wasn't good with children and the statement was meaningless to his son at the time.

Now those words mean everything and he wishes his father were alive to discuss them. Yet time only moves in one direction and not one second can be called back, no matter how badly we want it.

The squeak of the bathroom door interrupts his nightly meditation on the duality of love and loss.

He stands motionless, surrounded by the rising mist like a man lost in the fog, waiting for something to happen.

A moment later, the door closes again.

He turns off the water, grabs a towel from the rack. He steps out of the shower.

He's drying his hair when he notices the fogged mirror.

I love you, his wife has written in the condensation.

He wonders if something happened in her session with the therapist he refuses to see.

Maybe there was a breakthrough.

Maybe things are getting better.

Maybe they'll be able move on with their lives soon.

Or maybe she's just desperate to feel like there's some kind of hope left for them.

×

WHEN HE ENTERS THE ROOM, his wife is in bed, under the covers, facing away from him.

He is very quiet and does not turn on the light.

He dresses for bed, slips under the covers, and listens to his wife's deep, troubled breathing.

Eventually, he falls asleep, but only because he ran and repeated the names.

If he hadn't, he'd be up all night.

Not that his sleep will be easy.

There are still the nightmares.

There are still the memories.

These ghosts live in his mind and in his heart, speaking to him, telling him every lie and every truth he doesn't want to hear.

×

Sometime after midnight, he opens his eyes from a sleep so shallow it is worthless.

His wife is not next to him.

He crawls out from under the covers, muttering as his feet touch the cold wooden floor.

He puts on his slippers and robe.

He moves through the dark house, each step soft, as quiet as can be. He knows where every loose floorboard awaits and he avoids them with ease.

He stops at the end of the hallway, across from the kitchen where his wife is sitting on a barstool at the island.

She holds a photograph, clutching it to her chest.

She has lit a candle but otherwise there is no light.

His cup of hot chocolate is on the counter, forgotten.

He watches his wife cry and he considers his options.

A moment passes.

He returns to bed.

She doesn't need to hear his excuses and he couldn't find the words even if she did.

IN THE MORNING, THE DAYLIGHT sneaks past the curtains and burns his eyelids. He rolls over.

His wife is gone.

The school where she teaches is a forty-minute drive and she leaves before he knows a new day has arrived.

She'll be back.

She always comes back, although most days she doesn't want to return to the house, to the neighborhood, to the town.

He knows this because he knows her.

She wants to sell the house, but he won't hear of it.

Why does he insist they stay in a place so alive with so many painful memories?

Maybe because their neighbors understand the pain.

They understand the grief.

They understand the anger.

Even if they don't truly understand.

Everyone in this neighborhood has lost someone: a son or daughter or close friend.

They've all memorized the names of the dead.

Benjamin, Amanda, Susan, Michael, Andy, Beth, Lauren, David.

That's why he needs to stay.

If they were to leave, he and his wife would be alone with their demons.

Here they can be haunted with everyone else.

As he lies in bed watching the sun slash a path across the room, he thinks about their only son.

Benjamin was the first to vanish into the woods, but he would not be the last.

×

In the months prior to Benjamin's death there had been a great deal of tension in the house.

When he wasn't with his girlfriend, he was depressed and locked in his room, playing music much too loudly, as if to provoke yet another argument with his parents.

He hadn't been accepted into any of the colleges he had reluctantly applied to, and he refused to see a therapist to examine the causes of his wild mood swings.

Anger to suicidal depression to irrational outbursts became the norm.

When gently pressed about his plans for after high school, Benjamin declared that taking more worthless classes wasn't his next step in life.

He wanted to be a rock star.

Or a movie star.

Or an Internet sensation with millions of followers.

Someone famous.

Benjamin said if he had to, he'd run away and make a name for himself all on his own.

But Benjamin was never going anywhere.

BENJAMIN WAS MISSING FOR NEARLY four hours before his father had any idea something was wrong.

He had been out drinking with some coworkers, a relatively new habit that might have grown into a real problem eventually, and he thought that might be why his wife was still awake when he arrived home long after her usual bedtime.

But instead she told him she didn't know where Benjamin could be, his phone was going straight to voicemail, and she didn't know what to do.

He was really angry again and he said we were going to regret not supporting him after he was dead…I thought he was just pissed because we wouldn't help him buy that car until he came up with a plan for the fall, but you know how he's been lately…He said he was headed to the river with his friends, but it's so late…You don't think he…He couldn't have…right?

He feared the same thing his wife couldn't put into words, and he thought of the river.

Something about that river had always bothered him.

Those waters are deeper and faster than they look.

He had warned Benjamin to be careful there, even when his son was just a toddler who thought the neighbor's shaggy dog was the most wonderful of all of God's creations.

He asked his wife to call Benjamin's friends, although it was the middle of the night.

Some of them would be awake. Drunk or high, maybe, but able to answer the phone.

He sat slumped at the island in the kitchen with his chin against his chest as if waiting for a jury to return a verdict.

It came swiftly.

Benjamin's friends had last seen him by the river around sunset, but they didn't know where he went after that.

He had been in a foul mood, and he hadn't wanted to leave with them, and they had finally left him there alone.

They hadn't heard from him since, but they did know his girlfriend had dumped him earlier in the day.

She was headed to college in the fall. She said it was time for a clean break for both of them.

And now Benjamin was missing.

Running to the river that night was the first time he had run in years.

His legs shrieked in pain and he had to slow to a shuddering walk.

The heat of a million suns beat down on him even though it was night. His skin pulsated.

The humid summer air saturated his lungs as he limped and dragged himself forward, huffing and puffing with every step.

When he reached the trail at the end of the road, the path cloaked in darkness, he hesitated.

The swaying shadows seemed alive with his worst thoughts and fears.

But he pushed on, his heart hammering inside his chest, and when he reached the river, he noticed the way the moonlight lit the water.

The way the light danced.

He searched for his son, but found no one.

There was a rope hanging from a low-lying tree branch, though, dragging in the water. The swift current tugged on it with invisible hands.

He would think of that rope when the nightmares came.

×

WHEN HE RETURNED HOME, HIS wife was hysterical.

He asked her to call the police, but he told her not to mention what Benjamin had said before he left to meet his friends.

He didn't want anyone thinking their boy might have killed himself.

There had to be more.

He was right.

×

TWO POLICE OFFICERS ARRIVED AND they said not to worry.

Teens stay out too late all the time.

Most runaways get tired and lonely and hungry and come back within days.

Benjamin was probably fine.

Don't worry folks, one officer said. We'll find your boy.

The police never did.

Three days later, the first body turned up, but it wasn't Benjamin.

Those waters are deeper and faster than they look.

×

He wanted to believe his son was alive.

Hope and faith were all he and his wife had left.

They hoped for the best, and they prayed Benjamin had run off to pursue his dreams, but once the first body was discovered, hope and faith were fleeting.

The Riverside Killer had come to town.

×

Each victim was found hanging from a tree branch over the river, their mutilated corpse bobbing in the fast-moving current like a bloated apple.

A rope was used to lift them into place.

Piecing together the little information they had, the townspeople realized the killer must not have secured Benjamin's body well enough and the water had dragged him downstream.

A rookie mistake on the killer's part.

That was everyone's best guess, and his mind would not stop churning over the facts of the matter on the night his running ritual began.

He started running after the third funeral, but he left the house not actually knowing what he meant to do.

He walked a few blocks before his legs switched gears into a slow jog.

His legs remembered what it meant to pound your energy, your rage, your restlessness into the pavement.

His legs remembered the sense of freedom running could unleash within a person.

Soon he was running every night, and when he was called to the path and the river by some force he barely acknowledged, he answered that call without hesitation.

It was his secret route.

It was his secret place.

Yet one night, when his wife asked how his run had gone, he couldn't stop the words from spilling out of his mouth.

He couldn't stop himself from telling her the truth of where he went every night, telling her every truth he had been hiding from her.

And now he still can't stop telling her those things, over and over again, though that truth is slowly killing her.

×

EIGHT TEENAGERS DIED OVER THE course of the summer.

Benjamin, Amanda, Susan, Michael, Andy, Beth, Lauren, David.

Then six months passed and no more names were added to the list.

Everyone asked who the murderer could have been, but all they had to hold onto was the moniker given by the media.

The Riverside Killer: another name no one in town would ever forget.

×

HE REMEMBERS ALL OF THIS and more as he lies in bed, wasting the day away while his wife is teaching her sixth-grade students.

He quit his job last fall after an ugly confrontation with his boss. No one has asked him to come back.

Instead, he spends his day drifting in and out of consciousness, reliving every decision, every mistake, every regret.

In the early evening he hears the front door open and close.

He opens his eyes.

His wife stands in the bedroom doorway, her blurry form almost shimmering in the setting sunlight.

His vision clears and his wife's beauty is stunning, and the lust that springs from within him surprises him.

She says she'd like to talk.

"We need to talk" are her exact words, a phrase that has never meant anything good, not once in his entire life.

She says she wants their marriage to work, but she needs his help.

He nods, but he's thinking: If you had called the police right away, our son might be alive. All those other kids might be alive. Maybe the police could have stopped the killing before it began.

Once again he refuses to see the therapist—he refuses without words, he refuses with a strong shake of his head—but his rejection of the idea doesn't seem to bother his wife the way it normally does.

She says she understands his reluctance, but at the very least he has to start talking to her.

They have to talk about something other than his nights spent running along the river.

She needs the marriage to work.

Their marriage is all she has left.

He agrees with everything she says, but he doesn't reply.

Later, when he leaves for his nightly run, his wife is sobbing as the door closes behind him.

×

Benjamin is dead.

He knows he has to accept this, has to move on with his life, but for now all he can do is run and remember.

Benjamin, Amanda, Susan, Michael, Andy, Beth, Lauren, David.

Maybe tomorrow will be the day he and his wife discuss where their lives are headed and whether they fit into each other's plans for the future.

But for now he runs.

Tonight, storm clouds are unleashing their cold rain in heavy waves.

He runs like the rain, free of the memories and the pain.

He runs along the muddy path in the woods and he watches the rain strike the river like a hailstorm of bullets.

He runs harder and he thinks: Those waters are deeper and faster than they look.

He runs and his legs burn and he wonders, not for the first time, if maybe there should be no tomorrow.

If he dies, he'll never again have to remember the memories he has sunk into the deepest waters of his heart.

Every night, he wants to run so fast that he leaves the memories behind for good, leaves them to drown in the river, but he's never fast enough to escape the knowledge of what he has seen and done.

He runs harder, his legs nearly tripping over themselves in his frantic urgency, and he repeats the names of the dead.

He runs and he tries to forget what his son said the day he disappeared.

He tries to forget that his son had wanted to be famous.

He tries to ignore all the ways, both good and bad, a person can become a household name in the modern world.

Sometimes a moniker given by the media is enough.

His son's body was never found.

He repeats the names of the dead, and the rain and the river whisper them back.

The river calls to him.

If he dies tonight, he'll never again dream of why the Riverside Killer vanished without a trace.

Why the Riverside Killer will never return.

If he responds to the river's call, he'll never have to remember why the killing really ended...

And why he has the nightmares...

And why he must repeat the names of the dead...

And what really happened to his son...

The waters of our heart are deeper and faster than they look.

MAMA'S SLEEPING

Someone had shoveled the crumbling sidewalk and Jacob was grateful for that small favor as he made his way toward the brick apartment building, but he was also fairly certain he should have called off sick like most of his coworkers apparently had. Temperatures in the teens, wind chill less than zero, and most of his stops so far had required him to trudge through two feet of snow from the previous week's storm.

He wondered again what he was doing with his life. This was no way to make a living. Not only was the pay significantly less than the vo-tech program had promised, but people genuinely seemed to hate him. Sometimes kids threw snowballs or chunks of ice at his distinctive red and white work van with the VeriNet logo on the side. Adults yelled things he couldn't hear over the drone of the engine, although he was surprisingly good at reading lips when it came to the nasty names he was called.

Jacob had spent time in the joint and he never would have guessed that "cable repair technician" might end up being the most despised thing he could be known for. Some days he felt like public enemy number one, as if people thought he was personally responsible for the lies the flashy VeriNet advertisements used to get suckers locked in for two years of substandard service.

That said, he had a job to do—a job he did appreciate having, given his record—so here he was, making his way past the battered cars sleeping in the snow valleys their owners had excavated. There were also dozens of vehicles still cocooned in dirty mountains of ice, either because they were abandoned or because no one cared enough to liberate them. This had once been a nice part of town, maybe fifty years ago, but now you wouldn't want to be caught walking these streets after dark.

Jacob entered the lobby of the apartment building. Three of the overhead lights were busted and a fourth flickered as if taking a few last gasps of breath before dying. The green tile floor was wet with melted snow. A trashcan overflowed with junk mail. There was a dark puddle that Jacob slowly realized was blood no one had bothered to clean up.

"Jesus," he muttered. He checked the work order one more time—J Smith, Apartment 6B—and he groaned when he saw the date the troubleshooting call was logged. Four days ago. Christ. Folks were usually plenty pissed if one day had passed before someone arrived to fix their cable, let alone four.

He started up the stairs to the sixth floor, taking care not to slip and fall on the narrow steps. His health insurance plan was useless and he couldn't afford a trip to the emergency room. Hell, he wouldn't be able to pay his regular bills if he had to take time off to go to the hospital.

As he passed the door to the second floor, he heard Mexican rock music blaring. Thanks to his time in prison, he habla un poco de Español, just enough to get by, but not enough to follow anyone speaking too quickly or a singer screaming over heavy guitars and drums. The song was probably about chasing señoritas anyway; most of that music was in his experience. Nothing wrong with that. He loved the señoritas very much. Who didn't?

The door to the third floor did nothing to block the noise of kids running and shouting in the hallway in a mix of English and Spanish and Spanglish. There were wails and piercing shrieks, the likes of which only children could produce, sounds that might be blissful happiness or profound anger or both. Jacob shook his head, wondering how the neighbors tolerated the commotion.

By the time Jacob reached the sixth floor, he was sweating. He located apartment 6B, knocked on the door twice, and announced his presence and his company's name, as was standard operating procedure. Then he waited to discover how bad his day might get.

Sometimes he was greeted with a stream of profanities about how late he was, how long the customer had been without service, and everything else that was apparently his responsibility and burden. That said, sometimes the customers were gracious and appreciative of his work. There was no way to guess which way the service call might go. Nice part of town, bad part of town, it didn't matter. You met angels and assholes in both places.

After a minute, Jacob knocked again. The scheduled appointment window was huge, 11 AM to 4 PM in this case, so it was possible the customer wasn't home, which would absolutely suck given the stairs. He would have to make his way back to his van, report to dispatch, and wait fifteen minutes before trying to contact the customer again. If there was still no answer at the door, he could log the appointment as a no-show and let this be someone else's problem on a different shift. Or perhaps he would be back tomorrow. You never knew how the cards of customer service might be dealt.

As Jacob prepared to knock for the third and final time, he heard the click of a deadbolt unlocking. The door opened a crack and a metal chain sagged in the opening. At first Jacob thought no one was there, but then he spotted the eye peering out at him, halfway down the door, nearly at his waist. The eye of a child.

"Hello, I'm Jacob from VeriNet." He tilted the ID badge pinned to his parka toward that watching eyeball. "I was sent to check on a problem with your cable."

The door opened further, enough so Jacob could determine he was speaking to a little girl. Her yellow dress was dirty and there was a smudge of peanut butter on her face. Her hair was in a ponytail, but it hadn't been washed in a while.

"Mama's sleeping," the little girl whispered, raising one finger to her lips.

This wasn't an entirely surprising statement, not on this side of the tracks where half the kids had no fathers—immaculate conception babies some people called them—and their moms lived on food stamps and state assistance. Sleeping in until noon was probably pretty common in this building, in fact. Yet Jacob was shocked by the size of the televisions he saw in some of the most dilapidated apartments in town. Between what those luxuries cost to purchase—or more likely rent—and the price of the services VeriNet sold these people, he wondered why they needed so much help from his taxes.

The little girl stared at Jacob and he began to feel uncomfortable, as if she had somehow heard what he was thinking. Those eyes were both beautiful and haunting, and they were not trusting.

Jacob forced the thought from his mind and returned to his standard script for these situations. "There's a service fee if VeriNet has to send someone else again for the same problem. When does your mother usually get out of bed?"

"I don't know." The little girl sniffled and Jacob realized her eyes were wet with tears. "She hasn't woken up in days."

Oh shit. Everything clicked. He had heard stories of technicians finding customers dead, sometimes in bed and sometimes on the toilet and sometimes in the garage with the car still running, but it hadn't happened to him. Not yet, at least. He took a deep breath.

"How many days?" he asked, keeping his voice calm and casual.

"Three. I think."

"It's okay," Jacob replied when he couldn't think of anything else to say. "Maybe she's just real tired, right?"

The little girl closed the door without another word. Jacob wasn't sure of his next move. He doubted anyone was home in the other apartments on this floor. They were too quiet compared to the rest of the building. His cell phone was locked in the glove compartment of his work truck, per company policy. And that little girl was in there, all alone, with her almost certainly dead mother.

Jacob was still debating what to do when the door swung open. He stepped inside and the little girl closed the door behind him. The living room was neatly decorated with shelves of books, several potted plants, two side tables with reading lamps, and a couch. There wasn't any clutter and the apartment smelled clean. The furniture wasn't fancy but it was well cared for. Maybe he had misjudged the people who lived here.

"Where's the television?" Jacob asked out of habit.

"Mama's room," the little girl whispered. "She has the television. I got the radio."

"Okay, just stay here. I'll check on her."

Jacob forced his best smile, set his workbag next to the couch, removed his heavy winter gloves, and entered the apartment's lone hallway. There were three doors. To the right was a bathroom and to the left was a bedroom where he could hear the local pop station counting down this week's hits. Straight ahead was the master bedroom.

Jacob's heart accelerated as he approached the bedroom door. He was almost certain of what he would find and he didn't know what he would do then. He certainly hadn't expected to be put in this situation when he left his apartment this morning.

Jacob knocked on the door. No answer. He struggled to remember the name of the customer on the work order, which he had left in his bag in the living room. A common name...

"Hello, Ms. Smith? This is Jacob from VeriNet. I'm here about the problem with your cable."

No answer. He knocked and spoke louder. Still, no answer.

Jacob turned the doorknob, stepped into the room. The curtains were drawn and he walked toward them, keeping his eye on the figure under the comforter on the bed. The sheets did not rise and fall. He didn't attempt to muffle the impact of his work boots, but the person in the bed did not react.

Jacob pulled the curtains open, allowing the blinding winter sun to flood the room, and as the light illuminated the bed, he was convinced the woman was dead. He didn't need to examine her any closer to be sure. Her skin looked like wax and she wasn't breathing.

Oh shit, Jacob thought, stepping out of the bedroom and closing the door. As he made his way down the hallway he did his best to keep his expression neutral, but he had no idea if he was successful. The little girl stood by the couch.

"What's your name?" he asked.

"Elizabeth. How's my mama?"

"You were right, your mother's sleeping." The words were a spur-of-the-moment decision. He saw a telephone in the kitchen. There hadn't been one in the master bedroom. He knew what he needed to do next. "Did I hear the radio in your room?"

"Mama says it's okay so long as I don't bother the neighbors."

"That's very smart of your mother. Can you show me your radio?"

"Okay, I guess."

Elizabeth opened the door on the left side of the hallway and Jacob followed her into the small pink and white bedroom. The radio perched on the petite dresser was a little bit louder now, but the music was still so soft the girl didn't have to worry about any neighbors complaining. Some teenage pop star Jacob couldn't name if his life depended on it was belting out a tune that sounded like every other song on the radio these days. Even the soft parts of the music were loud.

"Are you sure my mama's okay?" Elizabeth asked, her voice conveying suspicions that all was not well in her world.

Jacob knelt before her, wiping a tear from her cheek. He took her small hands into his much larger hands. He squeezed in what he hoped was an encouraging manner, and the sensation of her tender flesh touching his callused skin sent an electric jolt through his body. He released her hands and his face flushed.

"Everything will be okay if you're a good girl and don't make a fuss," Jacob said as he reached under her yellow dress.

Elizabeth's eyes grew wide in horror as Jacob's fingers looped into her cotton underwear and yanked them toward the floor. She squirmed backwards, but he grabbed onto her arm and squeezed hard. The struggle set his entire body on fire, sending more electric thunderbolts through every muscle. This was the burning hunger that had landed him in prison, keeping him away from temptation for several very long years—and yet his time in the concrete cellblock suddenly felt like it was so very long ago.

"Mama!" the little girl yelled. "Mama!"

Jacob slapped her across the face and shoved her hard to the floor. She landed with a grunt.

"I said to be good," he growled as he fell upon her. She gazed up at him in fear. Blood trickled from her nose.

The radio on the dresser beeped and a broadcaster interrupted the music for the first time Jacob could remember since 9/11. The voice on the radio was nearly frantic. Something major had happened, a catastrophe of some kind, but Jacob barely heard what the man was saying. He was too focused on seizing this opportunity.

"Be a good girl," he whispered, caressing the girl's face, smearing the blood across her cheek as she struggled.

Instead, she cried: "Mama!"

Jacob grinned. "Honey, your mama is dead. She's not coming to help you."

The radio broadcaster was speaking even more urgently, and this time some part of Jacob's brain heard the words, but he still didn't understand them. They made no sense.

Then a cold, dead hand gripped Jacob's shoulder and began to squeeze.

AN INSTANT ETERNITY

"In life there is not time to grieve long
But this, this is out of life, this is
out of time,
An instant eternity of evil and wrong."
— T.S. Eliot, Murder in the Cathedral

No one was supposed to be in the abandoned town. The escorted group of reporters, photographers, and cameramen wore paper masks provided by the U.N.'s media liaison team, and they wouldn't be here for more than half an hour. There had been no sign of any civilians when the four CH-47 Chinook helicopters circled the region on the way in and they didn't expect to see anyone on the way out. Only the insane and the sick would still be living here.

Stephen carried his camera close as he walked alongside Rick McDuff, a reporter whose career dated clear back to Vietnam. Nothing fazed him anymore. Stephen wished he could say the same, but he was merely a self-taught photographer on his first tour of duty outside his hometown and, even after several months of traveling to places like this with Rick, he didn't have the courage or the stomach to process the horrific scenes with a cold, clinical eye the way his much older colleague did.

They were passing a crumbling house when a hesitant movement in the shadows caught Stephen's attention. There was a young girl in there, wearing a dirty and tattered dress draped over her skeletal frame. Her skin was pale and her eyes were very blue.

"Rick, look," Stephen whispered, pointing as the girl ducked deeper into the shadows of the interior.

"The house?"

"No, the little girl."

"I don't see anyone," Rick said. He glanced at Stephen for a moment, as if to confirm he wasn't joking, and then back at the ruins. "They searched to make sure the area was clear, you know."

Stephen didn't reply, but he approached the doorway and peered inside. There was no one there and no other signs of movement or occupation, no indication of life at all. Just debris and the broken remains of a household.

"Guess my imagination got away from me," he said, not believing the words but trying to save face. Rick studied him closely as they hurried to rejoin the group, and that made Stephen more uneasy. He didn't want to feel any crazier than he already felt.

He hadn't expected to witness such horrible things when he took this job, but whenever he closed his eyes he was greeted by an endless parade of children burned by the bombings, grieving widows digging shallow graves with their bare hands, people missing limbs, and scenes of heartbreaking destruction.

Other people's lives echoed through his thoughts like ghosts. Every burned-out car in the middle of a street told a story. Every buckled building. Every smashed skeleton on a scarred sidewalk. Every mound of dirt by the side of the road where the nameless dead rested. Sometimes, during the worst of the nightmares, he couldn't tell if he was awake or asleep.

When Stephen was a teenager, his father had once drunkenly told him that death was actually a single moment of eternity and there was nothing you could do in that moment but accept your fate. If your time was up, your time was up. Stephen had thought his father was being melodramatic, as he often was while in his cups, but not anymore. Terror and death surrounded him, whether his eyes were open or closed, and he just wanted to go home to be with his family, to leave this land of destruction behind forever.

The group of reporters entered the old town square full of wild grasses and bushes badly in need of tending. In the center of the square was a statue of a soldier, but almost no one in the group paid the monument any attention. In the distance was the highlight of their visit to this town. Down the hill from them was a nuclear power plant with four concrete cooling towers on an overgrown island on a narrow river. Everyone murmured excitedly.

Everyone except for Stephen, who was studying the ruins around the town square, searching for anyone else who might be hiding and watching them. Insects buzzed around his head, nipping at him, and the sunlight cooked his exposed flesh like a skillet. He felt disconnected from the world. Everything around him seemed to be shifting one step away from reality.

I need to get out of here, Stephen thought. Or I might never leave this country.

At least this visit would be quick. Several times the group had been cautioned about the continuing danger from the radiation. They were also frequently reminded by their guides of how the United Nations had dramatically flown into the Hot Zone after the power plant's meltdown to evacuate the community, losing two helicopters in the process. One had exploded on the ground and the other had been shot down by a rebel's surface-to-air missile stolen from an old military stockpile, but in the end, hundreds of townspeople had been saved.

The anniversary of the heroic rescue was the prepackaged story for this leg of the media field trip.

Most of the journalists would run with it. Using the prepared news was easier than digging for something deeper, and in the end, you got paid the same either way.

The reporters stomped forward through the overgrown grasses of the town square to get a better look at the power plant, but this was as far as they could go. The road beyond the square was a live minefield.

An advance team had placed a row of tall red cones adorned with international warning signs at the edge of the square and there were also bright red flags indicating the locations of several mines just beyond the cones. As if to reinforce this message, thirty yards into the danger zone were the burnt and twisted remains of the U.N. helicopter that had exploded when it landed during the town's evacuation. Near the wreckage was also a pick-up truck that had been shredded by an improvised explosive device.

"Think you should take a few photos, Mr. Photographer?" Rick asked, scribbling a few names off the monument into his notebook.

Stephen understood the angle Rick had chosen for his report and he started snapping shots to illustrate it: the tall statue from a low view, the remains of the wooden fence that once surrounded the town square, and the charred framework of the burned buildings. When possible, he included the four concrete towers looming in the distance.

With the camera's zoom lenses, he could actually see the old power plant quite well. The island's native vegetation had already consumed the buildings and the thick vines would camouflage the towers before too long. In a few years, they'd simply appear to be some oddly steep hills on the river.

"Time to return to our rides," the lead media liaison announced in his thick accent. "As we take off, try to imagine what it felt like for all the towns-people who were rescued from certain death in some of these same helicopters."

"You get the shots you wanted?" Rick asked while he packed his notebook for the flight to the Green Zone base where they'd spend the night.

"I have enough." Stephen stood by the monu-ment while everyone else dutifully filed back to the street, which led to the field outside of town where the helicopters waited, their powerful engines still revved and ready to go.

He was the last person in the town square. Something still felt very wrong to him. Déjà vu, maybe, as if he had been here before. Yet he never had been. He was certain of that. Then he heard a voice on the breeze. Someone calling for him from the group? No, the sound was behind him.

He looked toward the power plant and there she was again.

The little girl.

She was standing in the middle of the street, her eyes wide with terror. She remained motionless a few feet from the ruined pick-up truck as if his gaze had transformed her into a sculpture.

Stephen turned in the direction of the reporters and U.N. personnel walking briskly away from him. He had expected Rick to be waiting, but everyone was already near the top of the hill. No one had noticed he wasn't with them. Panic washed over Stephen.

"Hey, wait a minute! Hey, you guys! There's someone here!"

No one responded.

"Please help me," the little girl called.

Stephen hurried to the edge of the town square where the red cones and warning signs awaited him. He studied the street and the sidewalks lining it more closely than he had before.

Hundreds of mortar shells had peppered the area during the war and the holes left behind from the explosions had been filled with dirt at some point. Those dirt sections—some large, some small, some nearly the width of the street—seemed to be where the mines had been planted based on the red flags around the town square.

Stephen turned again to the group of people topping the hill.

"Hey!" he screamed, jumping and waving his arms. The group kept moving like they had already forgotten the town, vanishing from his line of sight.

"Please," the little girl whimpered.

There wasn't any time to waste. Stephen took a deep breath and slowly stepped past the cones and the warning signs, making sure his shoes connected with firm pavement. He was terrified he was wrong about the locations of the mines and every step made his heart leap in his chest with panic, but when Stephen reached the little girl, he released the breath he hadn't realized he was holding and he relaxed. He dropped to one knee so they were both about the same height.

"I need help," she said very quietly, as if she were afraid to raise her voice.

"Come here." Stephen took her small hand into his own. Her bright blue eyes were filled with tears. Her skin was tight against her bones. "I'll take you to the helicopters and they'll fly you to safety."

"No!" She yanked her hand free, but she didn't attempt to run away.

"Honey, we need to go right now."

"I can't."

"Why not?"

With a trembling hand, the little girl pointed at her battered tennis shoes, which were speckled with dried blood. She was standing on a slight mound of dirt that had shifted under her weight.

"I heard it click," she whispered.

"Oh shit."

Stephen stood and gazed toward the top of the hill. He saw no one. He could hear the rotors speeding up as the helicopters prepared to leave.

In his panic, he almost started to run, but then he remembered where he was and stopped cold. Between him and safety were all those holes filled with dirt, the red flags near the town square, the cones with their warning signs facing away from him. He was definitely on the wrong side of the safe zone.

"Please don't leave me," the little girl whispered.

"I have to get some help. Don't move, okay? Not one inch. I'll be right back. I promise I won't leave you here."

"Please hurry."

"Just don't move, I'll be right back with help."

Stephen navigated his way past where he believed the mines had been buried. His eyes were locked on the ground and sweat poured off his face.

By the time he reached the town square, the first helicopter had risen above the tree line. If Stephen were lucky, they'd fly his way and someone would spot him. Even if they flew in the other direction, he should still be okay, though. The U.N. media liaisons were supposed to do a head count on each helicopter, just to be safe. When they did that, they would realize they were one person short and they'd count again.

Stephen knew he couldn't depend on Rick to realize his photographer was missing since they had ridden on different helicopters at least twice today and there was no assigned seating, but one of the media liaisons would notice. They'd have to notice. Taking care of the journalists was their job, after all.

Stephen raced across the town square while two more helicopters rose into the sky. They headed south, away from the town.

"Dammit," he whispered, breaking into a sprint, pushing himself as hard as he could, his legs churning under him, his camera swinging around his neck. He had been a track and field star in high school, winning several races at the regional level and finishing in the top three for the high jump twice, but he hadn't maintained that level of fitness since he married and entered the workforce.

Stephen reached the top of the hill where the town's main street became a winding road that passed by a creek and the U.N.'s improvised landing field before twisting into the woods and continuing to an old highway five miles away. He started down the other side of the hill as the last helicopter lifted off.

"Hey! Hey, you idiots! You were supposed to count!" he screamed, running toward the field of overgrown grass and forgotten farm equipment. The helicopter continued up and then turned south, following the first three. Stephen jumped and waved his arms like a madman, but still, no one saw him.

"No, dammit! Down here!"

The last helicopter vanished over the hills, the sound of the rotors quickly fading away. Stephen was left standing alone in the field full of muddy boot prints, trampled weeds, and abandoned tractors. A candy wrapper blew past him on the summer breeze.

"Dammit, God dammit," Stephen muttered, rushing back to town. He topped the hill and was relieved to see the little girl hadn't moved. His legs were beginning to ache, but he didn't slow until he reached the memorial in the town square.

There he stopped and lifted his camera, focused on the girl, and snapped a couple of shots. If he didn't make it back, he wanted his photographs to survive and explain what had happened. He placed the camera on the wooden bench near the statue.

"You're going to be okay," Stephen called to the girl as he once again carefully navigated his way to where she stood. "Stay very, very still. I'll get you out of here."

"Please don't leave me again," the little girl whispered.

"I won't." Stephen knelt in front of her, wiped her tears away. "What's your name?"

"Lilly."

"That's a pretty name. Listen to me, Lilly. You can't move. Do you understand?"

She nodded.

"You heard something click when you stepped on the dirt?"

"Yes. The bad click. Like the one that killed Mommy. The one Daddy taught me about."

"How did you get here? Where's your father?"

"Daddy's a soldier."

"Does he wear a uniform?"

"Before Mommy died."

"What about after your mother died?"

"Daddy took me and my brothers to some cabins in the woods with some other soldiers."

Oh shit, Stephen thought. Her father joined one of the rebel groups.

"Then they went to fight the bad men and they never came back."

"How long have they been gone?"

"Since winter. I came here to find them."

Stephen thought about the last major offensive against the rebels before the truce, five months ago. That battle wasn't too far from this town, maybe ten miles, just outside the capital city. One last stand on the bloody riverbanks and small islands, a night of gunfire and explosions and bloodshed. He shot a lot of graphic photos afterwards, far too graphic to appear in the legitimate news, but there were plenty of websites that would have bought them if he had been selling. Instead, he had erased his camera's memory card at the hotel that night. He might have photographed her brothers or her father for all he knew.

"Mommy died over there," Lilly said, pointing. "We were walking to the market and a bomb in the ground clicked and she told me to get away real fast."

"I'm sorry," Stephen said. He put his hands on his knees to steady himself against a wave of dizziness. The street was so damn hot. The tar in the pavement's cracks was bubbling and the heat shimmered in the air like dancing phantoms. His armpits were damp and his pulse was racing; he could hear his heart beating in his ears. His fingers shook, just a little.

"Please help me," Lilly whispered. "Daddy told me not to move if I heard a click when I was walking. He said he'd help me."

"It's good you didn't move. Are you sure you heard a click?"

"Yes. Like Mommy's."

"Lilly, you're going to be okay. Trust me."

She nodded, believing him in the way children are trained to believe adults. Then she glanced around, as if she heard a familiar sound, and her body swayed and her eyelids fluttered. Her eyes bulged and rolled. Her legs bent at the knees and she started to collapse.

Stephen reached out, caught the little girl by the arms, and held her so her weight was still pressing down on the ground. Her eyes remained closed and her body shook and for the longest moment of his life, Stephen was certain they were about to die. If her weight shifted too much, the mine would explode and they'd both be killed instantly.

Lilly's body stopped shaking, but her eyes didn't open. Stephen continued to hold the little girl in place, her tiny body surprisingly heavy in the blistering heat. He had enough time to wonder if she would never wake up—a terrifying thought considering he was supporting her weight on top of a high-explosive mine—before she began to blink and her eyes finally opened.

"What happened?" she asked, groggy, like she had been awakened from a deep sleep.

"Are you okay?"

"Sorry," she whispered. "I got dizzy. I'm so thirsty."

"It's okay," he said. "I can get you some water."

But he couldn't. Not here. This whole area was poison. There wasn't any clean water anywhere, and even if there were, he couldn't leave this little girl alone in her condition. Instead he kept holding her and he didn't say anything else until she finally spoke again.

"I'm so tired."

"You need to stay still, but don't worry, you'll be okay."

Stephen's mind was running red hot. He had seen so many people killed by mines since he came to this country. Stepping in the wrong place in the wrong field, driving on the wrong road. Once he had watched from a distance as a U.N. bomb disposal unit attempted to disarm a mine buried in the middle of a playground. The men were blown to pieces. They had been pros. They were dead.

Stephen wiped more sweat and tears away from the little girl's face. Considering how exhausted she was and given the situation, he thought she was holding herself together pretty well. Better than some adults he had seen. Maybe because she truly believed there was a way out of the situation, some means to fix this problem. She didn't know the truth like he did.

"Do you know what kind of bomb it is, Lilly? Did your father ever mention that?"

Her eyes had grown glassy, but Stephen's words seemed to wake her up a bit. She whispered, "It hops."

It hops.

A hopping bomb. Stephen understood. Rick had called them Bouncing Betties. They were quite popular for the rebels in this war thanks to all of the Army depots that had been overrun in the early days of the fighting. There were millions of these things littering the landscape, hibernating under the dirt, just waiting to release their explosive fury.

Stephen remembered sitting with Rick in some hotel bar as the veteran journalist explained that a Bouncing Betty was designed to launch into the air after a soldier activated it, detonating approximately three seconds later so the explosion would rip apart a whole group of soldiers instead of maiming or killing just one.

Stephen felt his heart sink as he held the little girl. There was no way off the mine for her unless he could somehow get the U.N. bomb squad flown to the town—and fast.

He contemplated his options. He could start running out of town immediately and hope to find help. It would take him an hour to reach the old highway, at least, and he had no idea what might be waiting for him there. Certainly not a bomb technician. Maybe someone who might be able to call for help if luck was on his side. But they'd need to have a working CB radio, which was hard to come by these days. Cell phones hadn't worked for years and the landlines were all blown to hell. Where were the nearest communities supposed to be again? Ten miles up the highway?

Lilly would never last that long. She could barely stand on her own. How could he expect her to stand motionless for hours or more likely days?

His other option was to hope and pray that someone would just happen to come along, someone with the appropriate knowledge to help, or that the U.N. would realize he had been left behind and hurry back for him. But Stephen knew what hopes and prayers got you in this wasteland.

Besides, the media liaisons hadn't bothered to do the head count like they were supposed to before taking off, so his absence might not be noticed until tonight. And even then, who would guess he had been left in this godforsaken town? More likely, they'd assume he had flaked out like so many journalists before him when they faced the horrors of this war. Some of his colleagues might check for him in the hotel bar, if they checked anywhere.

It could be days before they understood something terrible had happened and they probably would never guess he had been left behind on this trip. Kidnappings and murders were so common in this country, they'd probably assume he was dead in a ditch somewhere and they'd wait for his headless body to arrive in the morgue.

Stephen thought of his wife and daughter and his life back home. Rebecca and Tracy, waiting for him. Desperate for him to return safely. He thought of everything he could lose by making the wrong decision, right here, right now.

Then another idea took shape, one so crazy that Stephen was sure it was the result of the heat baking his brain. Two competing versions of himself started to debate inside his head:

Could that work? Really? Maybe?

What are the odds, though?

What other choice is there?

You're fucking kidding yourself, Stephen.

Well, I have to do something!

But you don't know if the kid's right about the type of mine. Or what if Rick was mistaken about the way the Bouncing Betties work? What if the little girl's father was wrong about the type of mines in the first place? What the hell are you doing anyway? You need to get out of here before you die!

I can't leave her, I just can't!

The little girl whispered, "Please...I'm falling."

"Lilly, you need to stay steady for a little longer, okay? Can you support yourself for a minute?"

She wiped her eyes and nodded. Stephen released her arms, stood and stretched his legs, which were already stiff from kneeling.

She whispered, "Please don't leave me."

"I have to check something over there," Stephen said, pointing at the crumbling remains of a barbershop on the other side of the street.

"What about me?"

"Stay very still. Everything will be okay," he said, flashing a forced smile. "Don't move. I'll be right back."

She nodded, but Stephen could see how weak she was. Standing like that in the hot sun for even ten minutes had to be tough on her. She obviously hadn't eaten a decent meal in months and the water she'd been drinking was most likely killing her.

Stephen carefully made his way across the street to the ruined barbershop. He avoided any patches of dirt that seemed suspect and he reached his destination without incident. He didn't know for certain, but he thought he was probably outside of the blast radius. He watched the little girl as his mind spun with a million reasons why he should hurry away in the opposite direction instead of risking his life. He thought about his wife and his daughter waiting back home for him to return safely.

Stephen stretched his legs, squatting down, standing back up on his tippy toes, all the time watching Lilly. The movements came naturally enough. He had loosened these muscles thousands of times before high school track and field meets, although he had never imagined his legs could ever feel as old and heavy as they did today.

Stephen thought about his crazy idea again and the other voices in his head fell silent, resigned. He knew his timing had to be perfect. Everything had to be perfect. He also needed a lot of luck.

Lilly was frozen with fear, her eyes locked on him. Her legs were shaking badly and her arms twitched. She was about to lose her balance again, to pass out from the heat and the dehydration, and the mine would kill her where she landed.

She opened her mouth but no sounds emerged. She stared straight at Stephen, her eyes pleading for him to help her, to please do something or she would fall and she knew what that meant and she didn't want to die like her mother. Her eyes bulged and started to roll back into her head.

Before Stephen could have a second thought, before he could say a prayer or think of Rebecca and Tracy and have a change of heart, his legs were moving. He deftly dodged the dirt sections, his shoes hitting the solid patches of pavement he had selected on his way across the street.

Lilly's swaying became more pronounced and her feet were on the verge of shifting when Stephen slammed into her at his top possible speed. In the same movement, he grabbed her under her arms and lifted her off the ground. He bent his legs and his knees coiled like springs and he launched himself into the air toward the back of the pick-up truck, pulling the little girl tight to his chest.

Stephen's legs clipped the side of the truck and he tumbled forward, landing on top of Lilly inside the truck bed.

His life flashed before his eyes and Stephen waited what felt like an eternity for the explosion. Again and again his mind repeated the memory of his father talking about death. Right now, here on this abandoned small-town street, he understood his father has been correct: death was making a decision and no mortal could change the outcome one way or another. Death could claim whomever it wanted. There were no exceptions. Death was eternity and eternity was death and…

Time snapped back to normal. The three seconds were long past and there had been no explosion. The ragged photographer and the little girl were still alive.

Stephen rolled onto his side and checked Lilly to make sure she hadn't been injured when they landed. The little girl lay there, stunned, her eyes blinking out of sync. Her dirty legs and arms were scraped and dotted with blood.

Stephen gasped in a breath and pushed himself to his knees, tumbling over the far side of the truck, landing hard on the sidewalk. He lurched to his feet, stretched into the bed of the truck, and lifted Lilly into his arms. He carried her to the town square as quickly as he could, not daring to glance over his shoulder. He didn't stop until he had passed the war monument.

By then Stephen's entire body was trembling as the adrenaline rush came to a sudden end, and he gently placed Lilly on the bench next to his camera. He leaned against the base of the tall metal soldier and stared down the street. There were metal prongs sticking out of the dirt patch Lilly had been standing on, but nothing had happened.

A dud! The damn thing was a dud! Stephen thought just as the mine was violently propelled into the air and detonated.

Even at this distance, the explosion was louder than anything he had experienced in his entire life. The pick-up truck flipped into the air as if lifted by the hand of God. Shrapnel rocketed through the town square, coming so close to Stephen's head that he could feel the superheated metal passing by his ears. The sound of the explosion echoed across the valley.

"Jesus," he whispered. His legs lost all their strength and he collapsed into the tall grasses. They pricked at his exposed skin like tiny knives, but he didn't notice. He didn't care. He couldn't believe he was still alive.

"Are we safe?" the little girl asked, one arm covering her eyes from the beating rays of the sun, the other arm hanging limply off the edge of the bench.

"We made it, Rebecca, we made it," Stephen said, rolling over and staring up at the monument of the soldier, which blocked the angry gaze of the summer sun from his face. That tiny bit of shade was a relief. Stephen reached out and took the little girl's hand into his own again.

"Who's Rebecca?"

Stephen realized what he had said. "She's my daughter."

He pushed himself to his feet, his entire body aching. He felt like he was a million years old. He retrieved his camera, secured it around his neck. He glanced back at the burning truck. It was a miracle they were alive. In that moment of eternity, for whatever reason, death hadn't claimed them.

When Stephen looked back at Lilly, he saw she was already sound asleep. He could understand why. He was exhausted and the heat was nearly enough to knock him back to the ground, but there was no time to waste.

He wrapped his arms under the little girl and he carried her away from the death and the destruction that was her hometown. He would make his way to the old highway and from there they would search for someone with a radio. It was their best and only option.

While he walked, Stephen thought about his wife and daughter waiting for him in his hometown on the other side of the ocean. He didn't want to consider the long road awaiting the little girl. Her journey was just beginning and she had no family, no community. She was trapped in a nation torn apart by war.

But right now none of that mattered. She needed doctors, she needed medicine, she needed clean water and a safe place to sleep. If she didn't get medical treatment soon, her lack of family and a stable homeland wouldn't be much of a problem for her. The dead didn't really care about such things.

Stephen would shepherd the little girl to safety and then he'd secure a seat on the first flight home, even if it meant quitting his job to depart early. He desperately hoped he could leave his haunted memories among the overgrown fields and burned towns and the rivers that occasionally ran dark red with blood.

Death had given him a second chance and he didn't intend to waste it.

Yet for the rest of his life, whenever Stephen closed his eyes, he would see the little girl standing under the hot afternoon sun in the middle of the street, all alone in the abandoned town on the hill overlooking the nuclear power plant. He would never forget Lilly standing in her tattered white dress, frozen in place, her eyes wide and pleading for his help.

That image would haunt Stephen until the end of his natural life, until the moment when eternity returned to claim what it was owed.

WHERE SUNLIGHT SLEEPS

EVERY SATURDAY, HIS LITTLE BOY awakens with the rising sun.

The middle-aged widower is already awake in his own bedroom down the hall. He has barely slept in the six months since his wife's tragic accident ripped her from their lives, breaking his heart and devastating his little boy, but he remains in bed and waits for the day to begin. What else can he do?

He hears his son's bedroom door creak open. He closes his eyes and pretends to be asleep. He hopes his son will not speak the words he always speaks on Saturday mornings, but the man's heart knows better.

"Daddy?" his little boy whispers.

The man blinks his eyes open, as if he's just waking up, and he forces a big smile for his son who stands in the doorway in his pajamas. The August sunlight sneaks around the curtains, washing across his little boy's angelic face. The father smiles even though he's frozen inside. He smiles and he hopes today won't be like every other Saturday for the last six months.

"Good morning, Timothy," he says.

"Mornin', Daddy. Can we go on the Mommy Tour?"

The father wants to sigh, but he holds his smile. This is what their therapist, Dr. Linda Madison, has advised him to do.

"Yes, of course. Give me ten minutes to get ready."

His son's smile widens as the little boy bounds back to his bedroom.

The father's smile fades into a grimace. He dresses in silence.

THE FATHER CAREFULLY PULLS OVER to the side of the road and puts the car in park. His son sits in the booster seat in the back, still smiling and following every word of the narrative his father tells every week. Timothy never loses interest or gets bored.

"I would drop her off there and she would go in through those doors," the man says, pointing across the street toward the black and silver office building.

His son nods.

"Then I would drive across town to my work, but at five o'clock I would return here to pick her up and we'd drive home together to make dinner."

The man continues with the story, but his mind is elsewhere. Sometimes he imagines someone has placed a camera across the road to photograph this spot every Saturday. What would that person think of this same car with the same occupants making the same motions, having the same conversation, every week? The seasons have changed, from late winter to spring to summer, but the car appears to be eternal. Is this an echo of some past event? Are the passengers simply shadowy ghosts?

"Do you want me to show you where I met your mother?" the father asks, as he does every week.

The answer is always the same.

WEAK AND WOUNDED

×

THE MALL HAS CHANGED CONSIDERABLY in the ten years since the man and his future wife came here on a blind date. The food court where they shared the first of many frozen yogurts has since been torn down, replaced by teenager specialty boutiques with strange names like Wet Seal and Hollister. The man isn't sure what those stores sell.

The man walks his son to the new and improved food court, which was built on the site of the old movie theater on the other side of the mall. He's grateful there aren't many people around yet.

"Here is the table where we met after Uncle Henry arranged for us to go on our first date."

This orange and blue table under the wide skylight is not the same table, but it serves the purpose for the story. The table is near the Starbucks kiosk that replaced the frozen yogurt stand from the old food court.

"Why did Uncle Henry do that?" his son asks for the twenty-fourth time.

"Because your mother was a friend of Aunt Alicia, and Aunt Alicia thought your mother and I could be great friends if we met. She was right about that, wasn't she?"

"You and Mommy were best friends, Daddy?"

"After you, she was my best friend in the whole wide world, kiddo."

As if on cue, his son says: "Okay, I want to see where you asked Mommy to marry you."

Dr. Linda said the so-called Mommy Tour would help Timothy heal by allowing him to connect with a side of his mother he didn't know. The doctor never hinted this could become a weekly obsession for the grieving boy.

When the father questioned her about this development, she replied: "Sometimes kids dig these holes inside themselves and hide their feelings there, often bad feelings they're scared of. A colleague of mine calls this the place where sunlight sleeps. Your son will need your assistance to find that sunlight."

"What does that mean?" the man asked, confused and tired.

"Well, if your son wants to take the Mommy Tour every week, it's because he's digging at something inside himself. Take your son and let him talk. Eventually, you'll learn something new about him and he'll learn something new about himself, and he will open up and reveal what he's been hiding."

The man didn't understand what the doctor was saying, but he would do anything to help his son, so the Mommy Tour continued like clockwork, every week, even after it began to feel like one of the circles of Dante's Hell for the man.

THE MAN SLOWS THE CAR to a stop near the curve in the dirt road. This state park has 40,000 acres of forest, but there was one trail in particular the man and his future wife liked the best when they hiked together the summer they first met. Being young and in love, they did certain things just out of sight of this trail that are not, for obvious reasons, mentioned on the Mommy Tour.

"Okay, Timothy, watch your step," the father says as he leads his son by the hand.

To get to Lover's Lookout (as the kids referred to the area when the man was a teenager) or to Scenic View Point (as the park guidebooks have always called it), you technically had to hike a three-mile trail from the park's Visitor Center.

That trail is rated for hikers of all ages, but there is also an off-limits park ranger access road that brings you within a hundred yards of the scenic view, saving the extended hike. Most people have no idea the dirt road exists, but it's been a lifesaver for the man these last six months. Making the full three-mile hike each way every Saturday probably would have broken him. He has so many powerful memories locked away everywhere in his life, just waiting for him to step on them like a landmine, but some of the most powerful were formed in this state park.

The boy asks, "Is this how you and Mommy came here?"

"Yes, all the time," the man lies. If he told his son about the real Scenic View Trail, they'd have to hike it every Saturday and he no longer has the heart to do that.

The undergrowth in this area isn't hard to push through and soon the man and his son are traveling along a narrow deer path. The sun slices through openings in the thick tree canopy, sending bright beams of light across the ground.

As far as the man knows, no one else uses this shortcut, which means there's never anyone to bother him and his son. The world is peaceful and calm, and they're all alone with the sounds of the forest.

When they reach the actual trail, they're only a few paces from the area on the map labeled Scenic View Point.

His son smiles widely and yells, "Hooray! We made it!"

The man smiles, too. His son's enthusiasm and laughter are the only things that keep him moving forward these days, and they're easily the best part of this heart-wrenching Saturday ritual.

The sight from the clearing at the top of the trail is stunning. Hikers have an unobstructed view of the treetops in the valley below and the curve of the river off in the distance. A fine mist often fills the valley in the morning and the sunsets are spectacular.

It's no wonder the man and his future wife spent so much time here, drinking and talking and doing the other things they did back in the woods where the man eventually discovered the private shortcut he now shares with his son.

"Did Mommy like coming here?"

"Yes, she did. It was her favorite place in the world."

"Did Mommy come here the day she left?"

"Timothy, your mother didn't leave us," the man says, trying to stay calm, trying not to be irritated. "She didn't leave us. You need to stop saying that. She had an accident and she passed away."

The man takes his son's hand and leads the boy back into the woods. He hates this part of the conversation.

"But she might come home?"

"No, your mother isn't coming home. The sooner we accept that, the better. You know what Dr. Linda says."

The man expects his son to start crying, right on schedule, but even though the little boy's jubilant smile is gone, his eyes are dry.

This is different. This could be a breakthrough. This could be exactly what Dr. Linda was trying to explain to him.

"Do you have something you want to talk about?"

His son nods as they walk, hand in hand, finding the deer path and making their way back to the car.

"Go ahead, it's okay."

The boy is still hesitant, but finally he replies: "Daddy, why were you yelling at Mommy the day she went away?"

The father grimaces as they continue to walk. He has worked very hard to forget the day his wife died, the day the rage flowing in his veins over some trivial disagreement made him see the world through a red haze. The screaming, the shouting, the swearing. His wife telling him to calm down or he would wake Timothy. The way his hands seemed to move on their own to shove her down the basement stairs. The thud of her head against the concrete floor. The instant regret, the horror when her pulse wouldn't start again, and the act of self-preservation as he scattered some of his son's Matchbox cars at the top of the steps and called 911.

No, the man doesn't like to think about these things, not one little bit.

For many years he had dug a hole deep inside himself to bury his bad feelings, and there they had festered and grown stronger in the dark until the day when they consumed him in a flash of white-hot fury.

The man hopes his son will do better with his own life, but he doesn't know how to answer this new question, so instead he says nothing and the boy doesn't ask again.

MARKING THE PASSAGE OF TIME

TIME BEGINS TO CRAWL, MOVING so slowly that a single tick of the second hand on his watch seems to take a minute.

John stares at the TV screen, unable to believe what he's seeing.

Julie is crying and shaking as she fumbles with the phone, desperately trying to enter her mother's number but failing even though she's called her old home a million times before. Her fingers just smack at the buttons.

The anchorman on the eleven o'clock news is frazzled and he's stumbling over his words.

This isn't right at all.

John can't hear the man's cracking voice anymore. All he can hear is a voice in his head, a voice he hasn't heard in years, a voice that asks: Have you ever considered how we measure the passage of time?

Somehow that breaks John's will, makes him want to cry — he knows they're probably going to die. Alone and in the dark. Somehow he knows life always comes to that moment of being alone, trapped in the dark. For everyone, everywhere, when time catches up and claims what it is due.

There are colorful graphics on the television screen, leftovers from just minutes before when their world wasn't ending.

People are running around the studio behind the anchorman and the female co-anchor who is speaking into her cell phone, even though she must know they're still on the air. A spotlight falls from the rafters, sparks fly. The camera pans to the right, as if the cameraman gave it a shove before fleeing, and the television screen shows the production staff scrambling in a frenzy.

Time is moving very quickly in that studio, but for John and Julie in their two-bedroom apartment, time is moving oh so slowly.

"How can it be busy?" Julie screams, dropping the phone. She must have gotten the numbers right after all.

And that scream gets John moving. He knows there's only a matter of minutes and there isn't much they can do, but they have to do what they can. They have to try to survive.

"We need to get this place prepared," he says, rolling out of bed.

"I have to call my mother. I have to..." She stutters and cries and it's clear she won't be able to help.

John runs to the hall closet and throws open the door. He grabs the staple gun, duct tape, and sheets of plastic he has stored on the top shelf ever since the night his father gave him a list of supplies to always have on hand for the end of the world. That advice was the ramblings of a crazy man, yet here John is, trapped in the sprinting present, needing these materials just like his father said he would.

John staples the plastic sheets over the windows and the front door of the apartment. He rips long strips of duct tape, the tape screaming, and he uses the strips to secure the edges of the plastic and cover the holes created by the staples.

Outside there is chaos — screeching of tires, cars colliding, sirens, gunshots — but John does not stop. Time is moving way too fast for him to waste a second.

When John is finished sealing the door and the windows, he returns to the bedroom.

"We need to get into the bathroom," he tells his wife.

Julie is still sitting on the bed, holding the phone. There is no dial tone. The television screen has turned into a hissing static. How could things fall apart so quickly? Jimmy Fallon should be on the television, not static.

"What's the point?" Julie asks.

"We have to try."

She reluctantly slides out from under the covers and John leads her by the hand to the guest bathroom across the hall. He turns on the light and closes the door, locks it, as if that will somehow help. The space is smaller than a prison cell, but it's nice enough for what it is.

Within a few minutes John has another plastic sheet stapled and taped over the door and the vent in the ceiling. There are no windows. These are all interior walls. This is as far away from the outside as they can get.

"We might be okay," John whispers.

Julie doesn't say anything. From the look on her face, John knows she has realized the end is really here. The lack of a dial tone and the television cutting to static was enough to convince her. This is where the ride known as humankind stops and everyone gets off.

But he isn't giving up. Not yet.

Maybe there's still a chance that they — they being the people who are supposed to be in charge — can stop this madness, can save everyone.

"We just need enough time," Julie whispers.

"My father once asked me a weird question," John replies. He's sitting on the toilet seat. Julie's in the tub, her knees pulled to her chest.

Julie says: "Have you ever considered how we measure the passage of time?"

Of course she knows the question. They've been married long enough that she has heard all of John's stories at least once, many of them twice or more—even the ones he doesn't realize she knows.

Now a memory echoes loud and clear in the front of John's mind: his father speaking on the phone. This conversation took place before his father committed suicide after saying the last semi-coherent things he would ever say, giving the last speech of his life:

Johnny, have you ever considered how we measure the passage of time? Early on in life, it's counting the days until the school year is done so we can run and play all summer. Then we grow and move on to slightly more important transitions: elementary school to middle school, middle school to high school. We note our first kiss, file it away in some part of our brain that'll most likely never forget until we get too old and it can't help forgetting. If we're sober, we can recite all the details of our first time in the backseat of a car with a girl. We clearly remember the thrill of the last week of high school and we compare that to the terror and excitement of the last week of college. These two events sound so similar, yet we remember and experience them differently. And it's all because of time. After college, we work toward promotions or better jobs. We marry. We settle down. We still look forward to summer, but now that escape is only two weeks, sometimes only one; sometimes there is no break. We slip into a routine, like a man in the hospital slipping into a coma. Life becomes regimented and we no longer monitor time through our own experiences and goals, but through the lives of others. Our child's first day of school. His first bike. Her first doll house. His first week at summer camp. Her first day at band camp. His championship baseball game. Her first date. His graduation from high school. Her last day home before leaving for college. Then eventually their new families, young and sweet and beautiful and naive. We mark the passage of time through other lives… but what do we do when those lives are gone?

His father rambled like that on the phone for much of the night, the same night he told his son how to prepare for the coming end of the world, and

John humored his father because he knew no one else would, not recognizing these were truly desperate words from a desperate man. His father loved giving speeches, he loved his conspiracy theories, and he may have sounded crazy to anyone else, but John understood that his father simply liked to talk. Lecturing. Giving instruction about something important.

That night, after saying goodbye to his son and hanging up the phone, John's father shot himself in the head, and he never spoke again.

But his words live on. John can still recite his father's last speech with stunning clarity — although he doesn't realize it. Sometimes John talks in his sleep and his father's last rambling words are what he says. Sometimes his night talking wakes Julie and she's terrified to hear her dead father-in-law speaking with her husband's lips. She never dares tell John in the morning what she's heard him say so many times.

And now John remembers the words oh too well and he wants to know how much time they have left because time is slowing again. It's dragging along, millisecond after millisecond.

The light above the mirror dies without any fanfare.

"How did we let this happen?" Julie whispers.

John can hear his wife quietly sobbing.

Time passes. Nothing is said.

John thinks about everything they will lose in a matter of minutes if the news was correct.

He's terrified and his brain locks. He's frozen on a single thought: How long will summer last this year?

There are so many regrets. Too many to count. If only the end would come quicker, at least then he wouldn't have to think so damn much.

But that's all he has time to do, so John sits in the dark and he thinks. He listens to his wife sob. He listens to the noise outside, which has finally grown loud enough to penetrate the walls of the apartment building.

There is screaming outside, and John wonders when it will stop.

"Are we going to be okay?" Julie asks.

John has no idea why she asked the question. She knows the answer.

He sits in the dark and he thinks and he listens to his watch methodically counting down until the end of the world.

He sits and he tries not to dwell on his regrets.

Time continues to crawl, moving so slowly that a single second seems to take an hour.

John wants to say something to his wife as the noise outside gets louder, but the only words he finds are: It's time to be counting the days until school is done so we can run and play all summer. All summer long with our friends.

They sit alone in the cold darkness and John gropes for Julie's hand and he says: "If only summer lasted our entire lives."

Then they wait for time to claim whatever it has to claim.

WALKING WITH THE GHOSTS OF PIER 13

ON THESE HOT SUMMER DAYS at the beginning of the New World, we're all walking with the dead.

The thought repeated in Jeremy's mind as he approached his destination, his tattered sandals smacking against the splintered boardwalk with every step.

It was a hot summer day. Sweltering, in fact. The sun filled the sky, bright and scorching, and the blinding light reflected off the sand like a field of broken glass. The wooden walkway formed the boundary between the beach and the town, and the planks were timeworn and weathered. Pieces of litter traveled on the breeze.

There weren't many people around—just a dirty bum here, a dirtier teenager there, along with a few elderly couples who probably had nowhere else they could go.

Most of the shops were closed, their heavy hurricane doors bolted shut. Normally the boardwalk and the beach and the small town of Penny Bay would be packed with people this time of year—couples on holiday, families with kids, retirees parked at Pat's House of Bingo, beautiful singles mixing and mingling on the sand all day before heading to the Bermuda Bar and Grill to party all night—but not today. Not now.

In the distance, Pier 13 floated on top of thick supports like a mirage. The summer microcosm stretched over the beach and the changing tides and the fingertips of the Atlantic Ocean. The wooden roller coaster at the end of the pier soared high above everything else, and although the ride's thirteen cars were racing along the track, there were no people strapped into the bright red seats. The padded safety bars only restrained the humid, sticky air.

Jeremy inhaled the salty sea breeze while the waves continued breaking and foaming and retreating as they had for millions of years. The water was blue and beautiful. The sky was clear, nearly perfect. This day might be the dictionary definition of summer perfection, yet there was barely anyone around.

Jeremy could easily recall what this place had been like years ago: the cascading noise of the crowd and the shopkeepers selling their wares, the drone of the small airplanes pulling advertising banners across the sky, the kids running and playing in the surf, the young couples holding hands, the scent of sunscreen and pizza, the soft-serve ice cream cones, and everything else that had made the beach his summer home as a child, when his family lived in New York City and spent the hottest days of the year relaxing here without a care in the world.

Everything real from those memories was gone, but their ghosts remained.

✕

There was a wooden ticket booth at the entrance to Pier 13 with an old-fashioned painted sign displaying the various rates for the amusement park. Locked inside was a kid Jeremy's age, his attention fully occupied by the cell phone he probably wasn't supposed to have with him while working.

"One please," Jeremy said.

The kid jerked back in surprise and looked up from his phone. His skin was acne-scarred, his arms tanned. His red uniform hadn't been washed in days and the expression on his face was tired and bored and maybe a little scared, too.

"One ticket or one All-Day Pass?" the kid asked. A rusted metal fan blew humid air around the booth and a battered radio sat by the ordering window. From the radio came the voice of a solemn reporter reading something off the newswire. The kid added, "We don't got many rides running. Most everyone quit."

"Why are you still hanging on?"

The kid shrugged. There was a bead of sweat forming on the end of his pimpled nose, near the metal stud protruding from a self-piercing that looked infected. "Don't got nowhere else to go."

"Yeah, ain't that the truth. Just one ticket, please."

×

Jeremy roamed the pier, passing the empty game booths and the empty rides, with the sound of the ocean forever in the background. When he finally found another human being, it was an older woman dressed not in a park uniform but a grimy Sunday dress. She was running the merry-go-swings every three minutes on schedule. There were no riders.

The woman sat under the direct gaze of the summer sun even though there was a bent umbrella on the boards nearby. She looked wired and tired, but Jeremy approached her anyway.

"Nice day, isn't it?" Jeremy said. The woman twitched and recoiled as if she had been struck.

"Is that you, Ralph?" she called, her voice raw and aching, her eyes searching wildly, as if she were blind. She looked right past Jeremy twice before she focused on him, her gaze like red-rimmed razors. "Goddamn you, Ralph! Why'd you bring the kids today! Goddamn you, Ralph!"

Backing away, Jeremy kept his eyes locked on her until he could turn a corner, and then he continued to explore the park, certain he would never say another word to the half-human husks haunting this wounded place.

×

But soon Jeremy found a man of Middle Eastern descent selling funnel cakes, and again he couldn't help himself. He approached the food cart, feeling sorry for the man standing in the blazing sun, dressed in his neatly-pressed red uniform. He probably had a family to support and couldn't consider leaving this crappy job. Where else would he find work these days?

"I loved these as a kid," Jeremy said as his funnel cake was prepared. He smiled.

The man didn't reply and Jeremy could see the worry in his eyes. He probably did have a family. Maybe he was thinking about them, wondering if they'd be alive when he got home... or if he'd make it home alive. Those questions were on everyone's mind when they walked out their front door these days, so it was easy for Jeremy to imagine what the man might be thinking.

The man said nothing as he accepted Jeremy's payment and handed over the funnel cake. Jeremy thanked him and dropped his change into the plastic jar with the word TIPS written in blue marker on a piece of masking tape.

As Jeremy continued walking to the real destination he had in mind for his visit today, he took a bite of the funnel cake and grimaced. He had certainly loved them as a child, but the sweetness tasted overwhelming and almost bitter to him.

He dropped the rest of the sugary confection into a blue trash barrel. A flock of seagulls descended in a pack, squawking wildly at each other, tearing the funnel cake apart and then turning on each other, sending feathers and bloody beaks flying. Their caws and screams and squeals pierced the shimmering air.

They had grown dependent on humans for their food, but there had been slim pickings lately and that dependence was leading to madness.

×

When Jeremy reached the wooden roller coaster known as the Screamin' Demon, he stood and watched it run a few times. Thirteen empty cars, chasing each other in circles, always starting at the same place and ending where they had begun their journey. Jeremy could relate.

The mid-day sun baked the roller coaster's fading paint. The metal cars seemed to sizzle. The peak of the first hill was at the very end of the pier, hanging out over the ocean, and Jeremy thought it was the most beautiful view in the world.

He and his brother Jason had ridden this ride hundreds or maybe thousands of times when they were kids. They had loved the Screamin' Demon, embracing the fear and the thrill and the rush that hit you directly in the gut as you barreled down the first hill toward the ocean. The next turn of the tracks was just out of view, giving you the momentary sensation of certain doom when all you could see was the water. Then the cars whooshed to the left, back onto the pier and climbing the second hill.

The sign over the entrance to the ride's loading line was blackened and scarred. The railed walkway was twisted and burned. Heavy plywood covered a jagged hole in the wooden planks. Yet the Screamin' Demon was still open for business.

The red cars were painted with bright yellow flames and grinning skulls and they roared by on the tracks, the grinding of metal on metal louder than normal. There was no one around to make any other noise: no shrieking riders, no chatting parents waiting on their kids, no teenage park employees pushing carts filled with ice and bottles of soda shouting about how refreshing an ice-cold Coca-Cola would taste. There were simply the cars on the track and the ocean below and nothing else.

"You want to ride?"

The teenage girl running the Screamin' Demon sat on a three-legged stool under a tattered yellow umbrella that had been patched back together with duct tape. She sounded hesitant and lonely at the same time. She probably felt the need for human contact, Jeremy guessed, just like he did. She was pretty in a simple, girl-at-the-beach kind of way with her blonde hair tied up in a ponytail, her blue eyes, her tanned skin.

She added, "Just two tickets."

"Oh, I only have one. When I was a kid, it only cost one."

"That's fine," the girl said, whispering as if there were someone to overhear them. "I really don't care. I'm not coming back tomorrow."

"Quitting?"

"Why bother? My paycheck is probably gonna bounce."

"I haven't been on this pier in a long time."

"Since you were a kid, right?"

"Yeah, my brother and I loved this place."

"Well, I hate it. My boyfriend and I are running away tonight."

"Where you going?"

"Anywhere but this shitty town. Maybe north."

"That's what Jason and I said."

"You queer?"

"No, Jason was my brother."

"Where's he now?"

"Dead."

"Oh."

"He was here last month, waiting in line."

"Oh." She glanced at the twisted metal. "I'm sorry."

"Yeah," Jeremy said, handing the girl his only ticket. She ripped it in half as he moved to take his seat. "I didn't really think the park would be open, let alone with the coaster running."

"You heard the President, didn't you?"

"Go on living, right?"

"Like nothing has changed," the girl said. "Like there's nothing to fear."

"You scared?"

"Out of my mind."

At the top of the first hill, the roller coaster paused for just a second, allowing Jeremy to take in the full view.

The sparkling waves of the Atlantic had conquered the world from below his feet to the horizon a hundred miles in the distance where the ocean met the beautiful, clear sky. The dazzling rays of sunlight formed an elongated diamond of fire on the dancing water.

Jeremy's skin tingled in the heat even as the ocean wind whipped past him. He could hear the cries of the seagulls and the crashing of the waves against the supports under the pier. He inhaled the salty sea air, conjuring a million memories of summers long gone, awakening a million ghosts who still lived here, and only here, and only in the summer.

"I miss you, bro," Jeremy whispered, and then his stomach rushed into his throat as the roller coaster roared down the hill, the cars screaming along the tracks like the demons they were named after.

He laughed like a kid.

He laughed to release the pain.

He laughed because he had to laugh or his heart would explode in anger and sadness.

When the ride was over, he was crying, and the laughter had been lost to the waves.

"YOU OKAY?" THE SCREAMIN' DEMON girl asked. "Oh man, you didn't knock your teeth on the safety bar or something, did you?"

"No, I'm all right," Jeremy said, removing his seat belt, pushing the safety bar up quickly so he could exit. He wiped away the tears with his hand.

"You're scared, too, aren't you?"

"Yeah, a little."

"We're probably safe, you know? I mean, they hit Disney in Florida the other day. They're kind of moving away from us. We might be safe."

"What did they do at Disney?"

"Man, don't you watch TV?"

"Not lately."

"Well, yeah, a bunch of them landed in a small plane and started shooting everyone with machine guns. Park security was useless. All of the news channels showed it live, too, from a local traffic helicopter. At least nine hundred people dead, lots of kids. The bastards were dressed in black masks and heavy jackets and when they were finally cornered by the Army, they blew themselves up."

"Makes the bombing here look like small potatoes, doesn't it?" Jeremy asked, considering the scarred sign, the twisted metal, and the plywood covering the hole in the pier.

This was where Jason died.

What had he been thinking right before the bomb went off? Had he been watching the ride following the tracks? The beautiful teenage girls in their bikinis? The seagulls swooping down for pieces of pretzels on the boards?

What had been going through his mind?

Jeremy thought about what it must have been like to be standing in line, enjoying the day even though you were packed in with hundreds of other sweaty summer revelers, waiting for your turn when...

Well, what happened next? It wouldn't be like the movies where the audience knows what's coming thanks to the music cues.

No, not at all like that.

There would be no warning.

If you were really close to the bomb, the force would shred your body instantly. You wouldn't hear or feel anything. One second you'd be alive and smiling or laughing or shading your eyes from the sun or wiping your brow or memorizing the curves of the hot chick in front of you in line, and the next second you'd be dead. You'd never have to worry about how your death would affect your family. You'd never have to think about the things you were going to miss or the things you would never get to do or see.

If you were a few yards away from the blast, maybe you'd hear the thunder a split second before the explosion ripped the life from your body, but there wouldn't be time for you to truly understand what was happening. A loud sound and then darkness. No pain, no thoughts.

But if you were a dozen yards away, you might be one of the unlucky ones who was wounded severely enough to bleed to death. You might hang on for minutes or hours, knowing you were doomed once the confusion settled. You'd be frightened and angry and you'd spend your last moments facing down every regret you ever had while wondering how the people you loved would take the news of your death. There would be a lot of pain and not all of it would be from the shrapnel that tore your flesh apart, severing your limbs or blinding you. Then, slowly, darkness and death.

"Small potatoes?" the girl finally said, studying Jeremy with fierce eyes. "Well, do you see all the reporters and cops? They're gone, right? We're old news. No one cares about the people slaughtered here because there's already bigger and bloodier stories to report."

"I'm sorry. Did you know anyone who died?"

"A couple of employees. One of my best friends. I think he went instantly. Didn't feel nothing." A tear had trickled past the girl's nose. Jeremy stared at her for a moment, at the tear, at her blue eyes, and he wondered if her eyes were bluer than the sea. "At least I want to believe that. Probably isn't true. I miss him. Sometimes I feel like he's still here."

"Yeah, we're all walking with the dead now, I think," Jeremy said and turned away.

The girl called after him, but he didn't look back.

"WAS IT WORTH THE TRIP?" the kid in the ticket booth asked as Jeremy exited Pier 13 and stepped onto the boardwalk.

"Huh?"

"Coming to see what they did."

"Yeah, I guess so. My bro is dead. Died here."

"I'm sorry." The kid with the pierced nose sounded sincere enough. "Don't worry, the Army will get the fuckers."

"Anything new on the news?" Jeremy nodded at the battered radio sitting in the booth where the fan continued to blow warm air around.

"Not really, just that the Prez is pretty sure this has something to do with the Middle East. Some new group of extremists with a crazy name. Makes sense to me. You'd have to be really fucked in the head like those desert-baked bastards to strap bombs to your chest and kill innocent people."

"Fucked in the head, or just really angry."

"Yeah, I guess. But angry about what? What could make someone so pissed they'd do this shit?"

"Maybe they don't think they'll be heard any other way. You never know what angry young men will do. It's a fucked-up world."

Before the kid in the ticket booth could respond, the radio crackled. He adjusted the tuning and turned up the volume.

An earnest reporter stated: "Earlier today, the Department of Homeland Security alerted police in eight major cities about possible threats to theaters. The threat is said to be credible, although no other details were provided and citizens are urged to not change their plans based on this report."

"This shit won't never end, will it?" the kid in the booth asked.

Jeremy shook his head. "No, I don't think so. Not for a long time."

"Where you going now?"

"New York City. I used to live there, with my brother and our parents. It's been a long time since I've been back."

"Just stay away from Broadway, man. You heard the news."

Jeremy didn't reply as he walked away, the boardwalk creaking under his steps. His face was coated in sweat. The sun was cooking him, burning him up, and the heat felt good.

He thought of Jason and the beach and the wooden roller coaster and the ocean and the summers of years past.

He thought about anger, and angry young men who feel they must go to extremes to achieve their goals.

He thought about Jason at Pier 13.

He thought about the explosion and the deaths and the future to come.

He thought about the last thing Jason had said to him the day he died: "On these hot summer days at the beginning of the New World, we're all walking with the dead. Love you, bro. Miss you."

Jeremy thought about all the people who might be attending a Broadway show this weekend, following the President's advice to go on living life like the world was just fine and dandy and not coming to an end all around them.

How could anyone look the other way so easily while the nation's body count rose so quickly?

How could anyone pretend everything hadn't changed forever?

How could they go on living their same old lives when so many people were already dead?

Jeremy walked and he remembered the people he had loved and lost. He remembered the ghosts haunting him, the ghosts he loved, the ghosts guiding him.

Some of those ghosts still lived on Pier 13, some only lived in his heart, but he could feel them everywhere he went.

He vowed to never forget his brother, no matter what happened.

Jeremy thought about anger and angry young men with a cause, and he walked with the ghosts, and he prepared himself for one last trip to New York.

A MOTHER'S LOVE

ANDREW STOPPED SHORT OF WHERE the hallways on the fourth floor of the Sunny Days Hospice Home crossed. Two nurses were gabbing around the corner and he didn't care for the people who worked here. The employees liked to chat with anyone they spotted, and at first he thought they were being friendly, but soon enough he realized they were just being nosy. Who were you here to see, what was your relationship, were you approved by the family—stupid, invasive questions.

His mother was alone right now, and Andrew hated when he wasn't by her side, but he was doing the best he could under the circumstances. He worked to pay their bills and keep their lives in some semblance of order as hers was coming to an end. He ran errands, buying her favorite cigarettes even after the doctor told her to drop the bad habit while she still could (as if that would make any difference at this late date), and he undertook any tasks that simply had to be done.

Once the nurses continued on their rounds, Andrew scurried along as quietly as he could, trying not to draw attention to himself. He remembered his first visit to this building, to a clean and well-lit office near the lobby where he begged the admissions lady, Miss Clarence, to please accept his mother into the facility, to please help him move her from his childhood home where he could no longer care for her properly.

Miss Clarence examined the paperwork Andrew completed in his thick block handwriting, and of course the first issue raised was whether he would have the money required, but he said he could cover the fees if they let him pay in installments until he could sell the house. That had to be possible, right?

It was, and Andrew felt relief wash over him, but then Miss Clarence surprised him with a bigger problem he hadn't anticipated: the lack of available beds at Sunny Days for new patients.

"What do you mean?" Andrew asked, his hands shaking. "Isn't everyone here dying?"

"Well, Mr. Smith," the young woman behind the desk patiently explained, "Our guests reside with us for as long as necessary to complete their life journey. We don't like to use the word *dying.* So final and crude. We like to say, they're *moving on.*"

"But how long until a bed opens up?"

"There's no way to know for certain, but if you'll agree to the payment plan we discussed, we'll call you as soon as there's a room available. Do you understand, Mr. Smith?"

Andrew had understood all right. He would be spending his entire life savings and then some for his mother's short stay in this place, but the people in charge were going to make him wait for the privilege. Powerful people liked to make the little people wait to flaunt their control over you. Andrew knew this. His mother had taught him well.

But still, he signed the financial paperwork and went home. What other option was there? He loved his mother, and she loved him, and he would do whatever she needed him to do. He understood there was nothing in the world like a mother's love. No girlfriend, no wife, not even another member of your family could love you the way your mother loved you, and you had to love her back just as much, maybe more.

Now Andrew was consumed by a different kind of waiting. The time of his mother's death—her *moving on,* to use Miss Clarence's term—was drawing nearer. He loved his mother so much and he needed to be there when her last moments on Earth came to pass. Being with his mother as she died, to keep her from being alone, was his responsibility.

Andrew walked down the bright and cheerful hallway, wincing whenever his shoes squeaked on the gleaming buffed floor. A television blared *Jeopardy* from somewhere, but many of the rooms were silent. The almost-dead didn't make much noise.

He neared the last doorway on the right, where the hallway terminated with a window overlooking a grove of trees. The sun was setting beyond the mountains in the distance and the sky blazed red and orange and shades of purple as if the air had caught fire.

Andrew stopped outside the door.

Could he really do what he had come here to do?

After all of these years of being his mother's only son, her best friend in the entire world, and the only person who loved her as much as she loved him, could he *really* do what needed to be done?

He had to, of course, he just had to, but self-doubt weighed heavily on his heart. He had decided on the way here that the best approach would be to think as little as possible once he was in the room. Forget emotions, forget humanity, forget the rules of nature, and become like a machine for a few minutes. Be cold, follow through, and then go home and force himself to forget his actions as soon as possible.

Andrew opened the door with those thoughts looping in his mind. The fiery sky bled in through the window and washed across the hospital-style bed where the old woman slept. Her skin was wrinkled and her teeth were yellowed. Her withered chest rose and fell. He leaned in to hear her wheezing. He could smell the cigarettes on her breath. The familiar stench was unmistakable.

Andrew stood motionless, just watching, and he realized he had to move or he would lose his nerve.

He put one shaking hand across her dry mouth. She snorted. He froze again.

Be cold, Andrew told himself, *be cold cold cold cold.*

He squeezed her nose closed with his index finger and a thumb. Her head tilted and her eyes blinked open. She was groggy and confused, and she rolled onto her side as if to get out of the bed, but he leaned forward to block her.

Reacting with surprising quickness, she reached up and clawed at his face with her brittle nails. The pain was intense. Blood trickled from his pierced skin. He hadn't planned on there being any blood; he hadn't expected her to wake up. He had assumed she would peacefully go to sleep forever.

Andrew doubled the pressure with his hand and fingers, turning his head away and closing his eyes to avoid her wild, perplexed, angry gaze.

Her torso bucked and she swatted at the back of his head with those calloused and bony fingers. There was so much life bursting from inside her in her final moments!

Then her body stilled, her jaw slackened, and the fight seemed to empty out of her as quickly as it had arrived.

She was silent.

Andrew kept his eyes closed as tears welled up. He had done it. He had really done it.

He slipped out of the room and hurried home.

When Andrew entered the tiny house where he had lived his entire life, he didn't bother turning on the lights.

How many times had he walked that hallway at Sunny Days, planning what he would do and then chickening out? How would his life change now that he had finally gone through with it? And how would he deal with a memory he knew would haunt him until his own death?

Andrew sat at the kitchen table and waited for the phone call. He would need to act surprised at the news. He felt hollow inside, as if his mother's cancer had actually been eating away at him, too, but he was sure his mother would be proud of him. She had always loved him so much, and he had always tried to return her love twice over or even more, doing whatever she needed him to do, going above and beyond to make her happy and comfortable, especially as her health deteriorated and the end grew closer.

When the phone finally rang, Andrew answered with a meek, barely audible: "Hello?"

"Hello? Mr. Smith? This is Miss Clarence from Sunny Days Hospice Home."

"Yes, Miss Clarence?"

"I'm glad I could reach you personally, Mr. Smith. One of our guests has moved on and we have a bed ready for your mother."

"Well, that's just swell," Andrew said, barely feeling like himself. "I'll go tell her."

He hung up the phone and made his way to the bedroom where his mother slept, where she had spent the last six months while her body weakened and death patiently waited for her to give up the fight.

Andrew loved his mother so much and he was relieved to finally have some good news to share with her.

STORY NOTES

BY BRIAN JAMES FREEMAN

SOME READERS ARE INTERESTED IN story notes from the author at the end of a short story collection, so this section exists for them. Feel free to skip this part if that sort of thing isn't your cup of tea, though.

That said, for those of you who enjoy a little inside information from the author about how the work came to be, stories can still be spoiled if you dive into the notes first.

If you've arrived here before reading the rest of the book, please do kindly flip back to the introduction or first story without further ado. Thank you!

×

WEAK AND WOUNDED

"RUNNING RAIN" WAS WRITTEN WHEN I was considerably younger and running a lot. Those days are long gone due to degenerative disc disease in my back, which basically means it feels like someone is twisting a rusty pry bar into my spine throughout the day, gradually ratcheting up the pain with each passing hour. It is not particularly pleasant.

"Running Rain" arrived in two parts. In the fall of 2003, my wife and I had been married for a little over a year and we were living in a ground-level apartment in Forest Hill, Maryland, not far from my work. I was running like a demon back then, usually after sundown as I've always loved running at night, and the weather one particular evening was very much as described in the beginning of this story. For whatever reason, that memory stuck with me, even though nothing eventful happened.

Then, about six months later, the entire story just popped into my head from out of nowhere during another run. My short stories tend to arrive in a burst of unexpected inspiration, and "Running Rain" arrived complete with an ending, some readers loved and others didn't quite follow. (I've received more correspondence about this ending than any other story I've ever written.)

When I got home that night, I wrote the story as quickly as I could and I was really pleased with how it turned out. There's a rhythm to the language I enjoy, and even after all these years, I liked "Running Rain" enough to put it first in this collection. I tried to clarify the ending a bit, too.

"MAMA'S SLEEPING" IS A PREVIOUSLY unpublished story written in the spring of 2016. The inspiration was a news article I had read a few years earlier about a rent-a-furniture delivery person who discovered a young child and his dead mother in an apartment. Most of "Mama's Sleeping," from the opening lines to the nature of the ending, formed in my mind before I even finished the article. I just didn't get around to putting it on paper for a while.

In real life, the delivery person was a good man who did the right thing for the child, but I tend to focus on the bad guys in this world, which I suspect feeds my muse a fairly unhealthy diet. "Mama's

Sleeping" features the worst person I've ever written about, as far as I'm concerned, but hopefully the reader doesn't realize how bad he is until the end of the story. In real life, some of the most awful people seem perfectly okay until it's too late.

One other note: throughout the story there are hints about what's happening in the world outside, but I tried to keep them subtle enough that no one would really notice until the second read.

"AN INSTANT ETERNITY" MIGHT BE my wife's favorite story of mine, and my favorite as well depending on the day and my mood, but it almost didn't make the cut for this collection. Not because my feelings for the story have changed over the years, but because deep down I know there's a novel wanting to grow out of this material.

I wrote the first draft of this story in college, more than sixteen years ago, so here's the short story in the meantime. Eventually, I would like to introduce readers to the untrustworthy pastor who offers his help in the old stone church down the road from the town, the abandoned amusement park kingdom of the ghoulish cult leader who calls himself The Blood King, and the people of the mountains who have been hiding from the rebels.

"Where Sunlight Sleeps" was inspired by a camping trip in the fall of 2008. Nothing particularly unpleasant happened to us that weekend, but a quick glimpse of a man walking hand-in-hand through the woods with his little boy resulted in this story. I'm sure that father and son had a wonderful weekend. I strongly doubt there was a murder in their shared past. Yet, thanks to a few seconds of watching them walk on a trail, I got this story, which I had a blast writing.

"Marking the Passage of Time" was written early in my marriage in an apartment very much like the one in the story. I wish I could say the world has become a better place since then, but I'd hate to lie to you.

×

"Walking With the Ghosts of Pier 13" was written on June 12, 2002. Crazy that I know the date, right? But writing this story changed my approach to short fiction and without that the rest of this collection probably wouldn't exist.

Here's what happened: my soon-to-be bride and I went to Hershey Park for the day. Like many people, terrorism was a thought close at hand that year and something I saw got me wondering what would happen if gunmen seized the park. The entire story, from the opening line to closing line, was firmly planted in my brain between rides.

We spent the night at the home of my future in-laws and I wrote the story on their PC tucked away in the old garage-turned-family room. When I was done, I emailed the file to Richard Chizmar, who was in the process of hiring me to work at Cemetery Dance Publications, and he bought it the next day for the first Shivers volume.

That turnaround time is insane for me. I usually don't let anything leave my desk without many rounds of rewrites and revisions. But like I said, this story changed my life.

"A Mother's Love" was born when someone asked me how far is too far to go to get someone you love the help they need. My own mother still hasn't read this one, but we'll see what she thinks when she does.

Here we are now, at the end of this collection. Thanks again for walking among the weak and the wounded with me. Grief and pain live inside these characters, but sometimes there's also madness and things much, much worse than a human being should know about. Please watch out if you discover yourself among them — or even worse, as one of them.

SPECIAL THANKS FOR PATREON SUPPORTERS

THE FOLLOWING PEOPLE GENEROUSLY SUPPORTED my Patreon page as of August 1, 2018 and made this new expanded edition possible. My deepest thanks go out to:

VICKI LIEBOWITZ, MICHAEL FOWLER, SHANON Cole, Brian Freeman, Louis Toth, Donald Shelton, Matt Schwartz, Doug Clegg, Mark Sieber, Dez Nemec, Patrick Bishop, Paul Fry, Richard A. Shirley, Keith Prochaska, Brian Keene, Robert Voss, Deborah Naus, Earl Robinson, Susan Pearson,

Steven McDonald, Robin Bruner, Todd Nesbitt, Julie H. Sullivan, Debra Torma, Adam Harding-Jones, Ethan Harris, Jonathan Sweet, Michelle Rother Lindsay, Thomas Millman, Russell King, Aaron Cohen, Pamela Taylor, Tami Franzel, David Jensen, Lisa Von Pervieux, Ann Waters, Robin Trischmann, Keejia M. Houchin, Alan Caldwell, Joseph Cameli, David F. Sabol, Rockie Suttle, Matthew Williams, Richard Platt, David Zicherman, Ron Weekes, James Coniglio, David Lars Chamberlain, John Fahey, Darren Heil, Kris Van Der Sande, Stephen Bamberg, Christa Jennings, Dan Newman, Roxane McLarnan Geggie, J Rivers Walsh, Elena DeGarmo, Bryan Moose, Dodi Miller, Todd Houts, Robert S. Righetti, Robert Mingee, Linda Przygoda, Veronica Ukas, Lisa A. Toombs, Jason Sechrest, Jason Canny, Lori Adams, Chris Nauta, Martha J. Davis, Sean Strange, Lori Reynolds, John J. Questore, Tami Kietzmann, Susan J. Darling, Michael Sauers, Gary L. Phillips, David Greenlaw, Twikie Simms, Ross W. Davidson, Rich DeMars, Larry Kinney, Michelle Floyd, Harold Dean Cook II, Deanna Kubisty, Janice Hill, Dorothy Lewis, Anderson Yee,

Special Thanks

Brian Nicola, Martin Garcia, David Pagan, Ronda Pennington, Daniel Zacharski, Philip Wickstrand, Joel McCandless, David McClung, Shannan Ross, Sue Wilson, Kim Meier-Carroll, David Ray, David Kipp, Kerry McKenna, Pamela A. Abel, Gary St. Clair, Keith Fritz, Heather Sage, Dominick, Steve Rider, Sean McBride, Levana Taylor, Michael Gutierrez, Connie Harrison, Shelly McGhan, Lynne Heinmiller, Kristy Lytle, Roger Terry, Kevin F. Wilson, Mary Grace Panebianco, Michael John Pawly, Susan Gray, Marilyn K Barber, Hunter Shea, Edward Roads, Stephen Herman, Ron Reese, Robert Brouhard, Tabitha Brouhard, Brad Saenz.

If you would like to learn more about the special rewards I'm creating for my readers, please visit this page:

https://www.patreon.com/BrianJamesFreeman

× × ×

SECRET BONUS HALLOWEEN POETRY SECTION

× × ×

"UNDER THE HALLOWEEN TREE"

I sat under the Halloween Tree
the creepy old tree at the edge of our farm
with a thousand limbs that could be climbed for hours
climbed right up into the clouds

I played in the brown and orange leaves
waiting for my brother to return
from his hike to the river with his friends and those girls
and I was already counting up the candy we would collect
as we went from house to house in town that evening

The sun dipped low in the sky
orange and red and golden and still
my brother and his friends and those girls did not return
but I watched for them knowing they wouldn't miss Halloween
not for the world
this was the most important day of the year
at least until Thanksgiving and Christmas
came around again
My brother and his friends and those girls did not return

at sunset so I ran home through the darkened fields
to tell my mother

I expected her to be worried but instead
she said, that's okay, I'll take you trick or treating
and I said we had to wait for my brother
he can't miss Halloween, it only comes once a year

But my mother replied, he's a teenager now,
there are more important things than Halloween
in his crazy, mixed-up, upside down world

She helped me into my costume that smelled like plastic
and then we went into town with all the other kids
and I collected my candy, going door to door
traveling the streets I knew by heart
skipping the apple houses,
concentrating on the candy houses,
but it wasn't nearly as much fun as before

And as I lay in bed that night
shaking from all the sugar
listening for my brother
and his friends and those girls
to finally come home again
I imagined myself in the branches of the Halloween Tree
and I wondered what my mother meant

"THE MIDNIGHT PEOPLE"

The Midnight People
came again last night
and smashed our pumpkins
in the driveway
leaving the orange
guts to rot

I've never seen
my father as angry
as he was this morning
swearing in the lawn
with the rising sun
lighting him up like a
raging angel

which makes me wonder
what will happen
when he finds out
I plan on joining
the Midnight People
as soon as I can

"TREATS OF THE TRICK"

The treats of the trick are simple
You must be more than a body inside a costume
You are not simply a boy covered in rubber
and foam and cloth
You are the monster, flesh and blood
You are here to stalk the land
Dining upon your prey
And dragging the poor unfortunate souls back to your lair
Where you will consume them in the hours
and days to come

The treats of the trick are for one night only
The monster you become is not real
The monster must be shed when his work is done
The monster is released just one night each year
And when that night is over
You wait for another year to pass
So you can practice the treats of the trick again

"REMEMBERING OCTOBERLAND"

The first time I traveled to Octoberland
I didn't know what to expect,
But my big brother was going
And I didn't want to be left behind.

My mother worried I was too young
But my father said, let the boy go,
There is nothing to fear.

My mother shook her head
Knowing my father was right
And she told me,
Just stay near your brother
And don't go anywhere alone.

The kids at school said the haunted house
Was a real haunted house
And the witch who once lived there
Was named Mrs. Witchenbones.
Oh, and she still lived there

In the attic
And she ate little boys
Who got lost in the woods.

These are the stories my brother
And his friends told me again
On the drive out to Octoberland
In my father's old Buick
Which smelled of beer and sweat.

We parked in the farmer's field
As the golden orange sun vanished
Behind the mountains to the west
And fallen leaves crunched under my shoes
As we approached the old farmhouse.

A girl in a mask sold tickets
From a wooden booth next to the big red barn.
My brother paid for mine
And he said mom would kill him
If I got lost in the corn maze.

He hurried off to the haunted house
With his friends, laughing and joking
Leaving me there in a crowd of strangers.

I chased after my brother
But he and his friends were already inside
The rustic house,
The main attraction of Octoberland.

I pushed around the other kids
And their parents entering
Through the narrow doorway.
I tripped on the dark stairs
But I kept moving through fake cobwebs
And the flashing lights and the props
Until a goblin leapt at me from a doorway
And I screamed.

There were too many people upstairs.
The crowd pushed and shoved,
Kids were laughing and crying,
The house so hot I couldn't breathe.
I ducked under a rope into another hallway
Past a mirror that made me look tall and skinny
And I found another set of stairs in the dark.

I climbed those wooden stairs
Searching for another way out
And I pushed open the door into
An attic full of darkness and clutter.
I kept moving and called my brother's name

Until I saw something move,
Someone hiding in the corner.
I wanted to scream as she rose up
Towering over me, growing impossibly tall,
And I knew in my heart she was
Mrs. Witchenbones

Her nose was crooked and green
She pointed at me with a scaly finger
And she said, turn around little boy
Rejoin the group while you can.
Octoberland is no place
To play alone.

And I realized for the first time
That my father could be wrong
And my mother could be right
Both at the same time.

LOST
AND
LONELY